TV Rex

Written & Illustrated by John Nickle

Scholastic Press
New York

To Jessie and Scott, for sharing my earliest TV memories

Library of Congress Cataloging-in-Publication Data

Nickle, John.
TV Rex / by John Nickle.—1st ed.
p. cm.
Summary: Missing his grandfather, Rex watches too much television and soon finds himself in a fantastical adventure where he stars in all his favorite shows.
ISBN 0-439-12043-8 (alk. paper)
[1. Grandfathers—Fiction. 2. Television—Fiction.] I. Title.   PZ7.N5585 Tv 2001   [Fic]—dc21
99-053214

10 9 8 7 6 5 4 3 2 1   01 02 03 04 05

Printed in Singapore   46
First edition, March 2001

The illustrations in this book were painted in acrylics.
The text type was set in 20-point Avon.
Book design by Kristina Albertson

One day, Rex was exploring in the attic when he found one of Grandpa's old TVs and some of his tools. Rex missed Grandpa and all the good times they'd had.

Grandpa was a retired inventor with great imagination. Rex always helped him fix things around the house. Together, they could fix anything. "You're a smart boy," Grandpa always said, "just like me!"

At the end of each day, Rex and Grandpa curled up in the big armchair and watched TV for one hour. Their favorite show was DEEP SEA HUNT.

When it was over, Grandpa would squeeze Rex's shoulder, turn off the set, and say, "Too much TV makes Rex a dull boy."

But now that Grandpa was gone, Rex was lonely. He wouldn't even LOOK at his own tools. All he ever did was watch TV. Rex never went outside and never, ever read anything, except the TV GUIDE.

One day, the TV broke. If Grandpa were here, he and Rex
would fix it. But Rex did not feel clever enough to try on his
own. The repairman came. He took the TV apart, rummaged
around inside, scratched his head, and said, "I give up!"

When Rex's glow-in-the-dark wristwatch told him that it was time for DEEP SEA HUNT, he crawled into the dark TV and began to cry. He cried and cried until the TV filled with so many salty tears that small fish appeared.

As Rex looked around, he saw that he was now deep underwater in a beautiful sea. He began to hear music that sounded very familiar. It was the theme song from DEEP SEA HUNT.

The announcer's voice said, "Today we will study the strange habits of the cave-dwelling Atlantic octopus with our special guest star...Rex!" Rex followed the music down, down, down through the cool, dark water into the octopus cave.

The music came from the Great Octopus's living room. Rex was delighted to discover that Octavia watched even more TV than he did...eight times more! Rex settled onto one of her cozy tentacles and together, they watched and watched.

Octovision made Rex tired, and after they had seen thirty-two shows in just two hours, he was ready to go to bed. Rex asked his new friend if she could help him get home. She swam off to her private chamber and returned with yet another remote control.

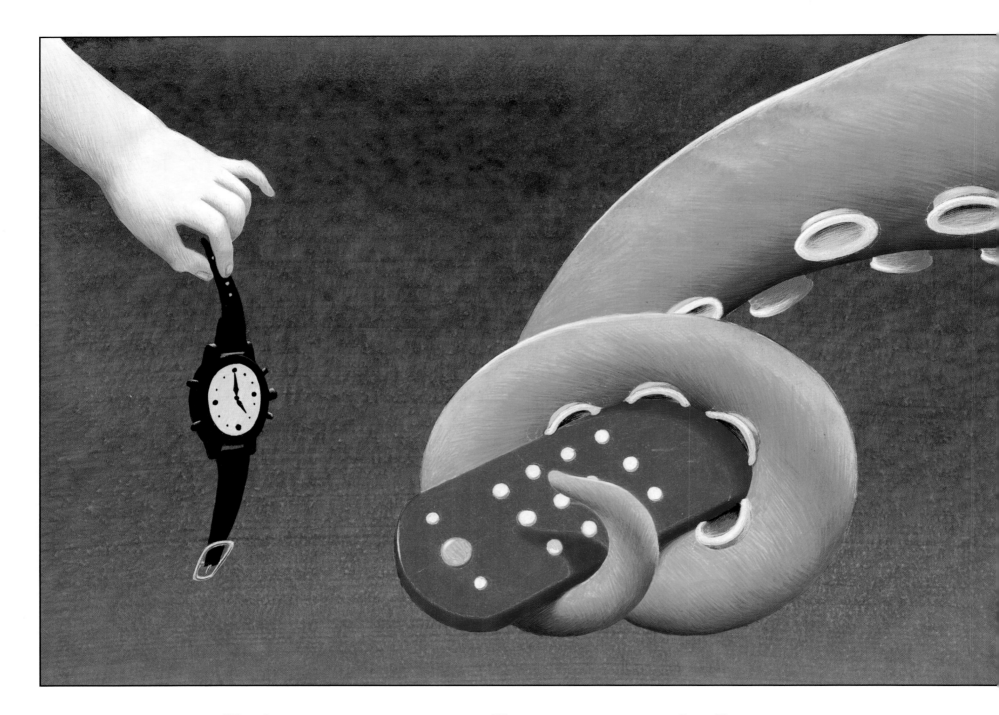

"Darling, to return home you'll need this, which I will trade for that fabulous glow-in-the-dark wristwatch. All eight of my remotes together do not equal the power of this one, the Superoctopower remote control. But be careful, press only the—"

ZAP! Rex was so excited that he started pushing buttons
before she finished explaining. Suddenly, Octavia, the
cave, and the ocean were gone.

Rex now found himself in the HARLY HOG CARTOON HOUR, one of his favorite shows. He and Harly had loads of fun outwitting two-wheeled weasels.

But when they saw what the dastardly weasel had in store for them, Rex frantically changed the channel.

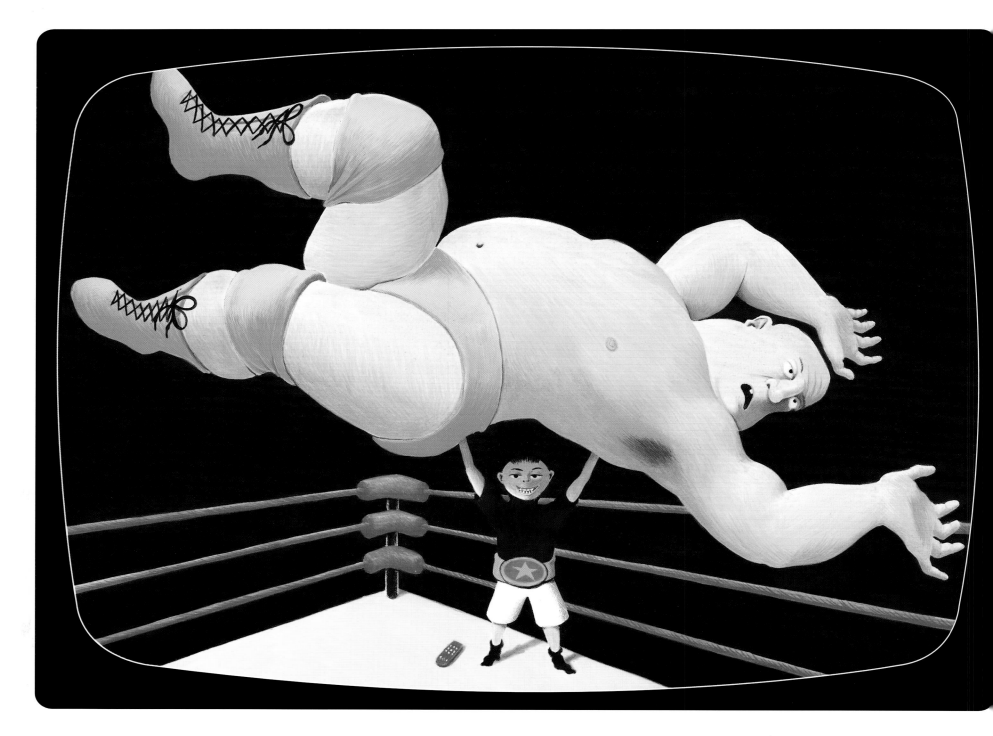

He escaped to WILD WORLD WRESTLING, where he was the champ.
Rex used his secret hold to defeat Vladimir Nokyerblokov, Toxic
Todd, and even Jacques Le Headlock.

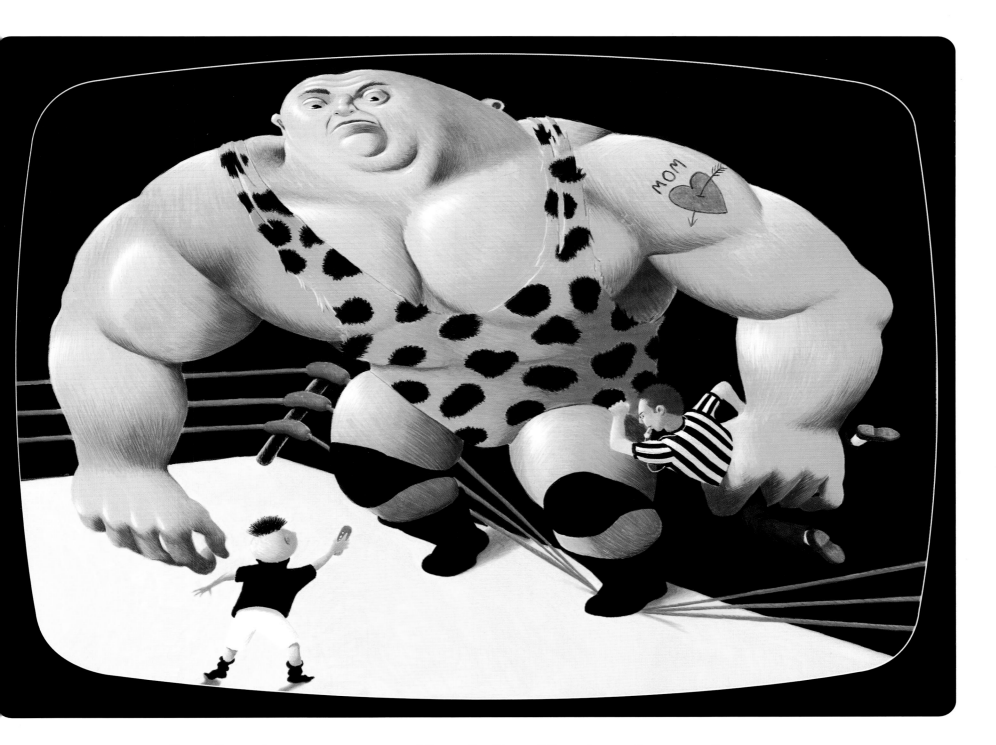

Rex feared no one except Mama's Boy Murphy, who was famous for his dirty tricks. Rex knew all he had to do was squeeze the Superoctopower remote.

In an instant, he was in AS MALIBU TURNS, where he was rich and drove a cool car. All the girls admired Rex from afar...

...except for Babs Amor, who wanted to get closer. ZAP!
Rex escaped just in time.

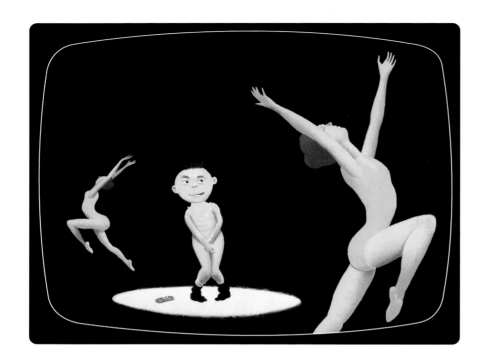

He zigged and zagged for hours, trying to get home. He had fun
for a while.

But Rex grew more and more tired. He had one last idea.

He zapped himself into DR. BLEEP IN OUTER SPACE. It was the oldest show on TV, starring the smartest man in the universe. As Dr. Bleep's assistant, Rex helped build Big Moe, a robot to rule the world. He was certain that, in return, Dr. Bleep would invent a way for him to get home.

But Dr. Bleep couldn't even bring the robot to life. He took the robot apart, rattled around inside, scratched his huge brain, and said, "Young man, I'm afraid this job is too big even for me. I give up!"

But Rex just would not give up! He was determined to get himself home. Suddenly, he remembered something that Grandpa had once taught him.

He twisted this cable and snipped that one, he pushed buttons and pulled levers, he greased the joints and oiled the sprockets. When Rex finally joined the red wire to the black wire, sparks flew...

...and the robot rattled to life!

Instead of ruling the world, Big Moe just clanged around the laboratory. He ate chairs, tables, and lamps. He ate beakers, bottles, and microscopes. When Big Moe picked up Rex like a bag of chips, Rex quickly hit the remote before Big Moe could eat him, too!

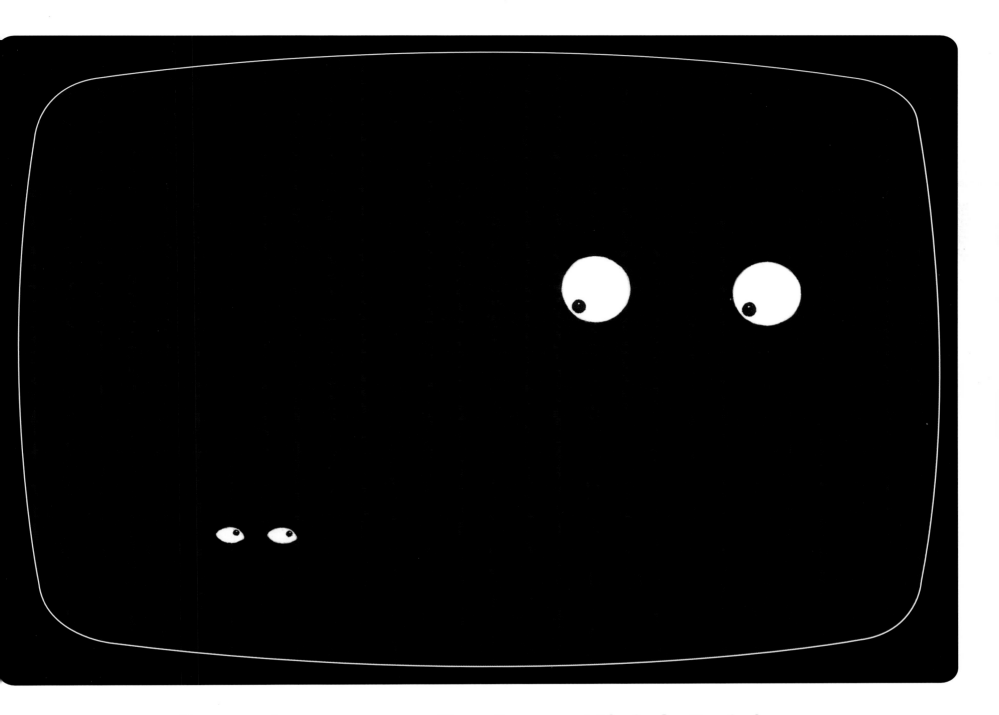

But something went wrong. Everything went black. In the darkness,
Rex felt cold metal clamp down on his shirt.

"Rex, how did you get in there?" hollered Grandpa, as he ruffled his grandson's hair. "I go to Florida for a couple of months and this place falls apart!

"Did ya miss me? I bet you were bored while I was gone. If you help, we can fix this darn thing in time to watch DEEP SEA HUNT. They're featuring that Atlantic octopus today."

Rex and Grandpa got to work and had the old TV up and running in no time.

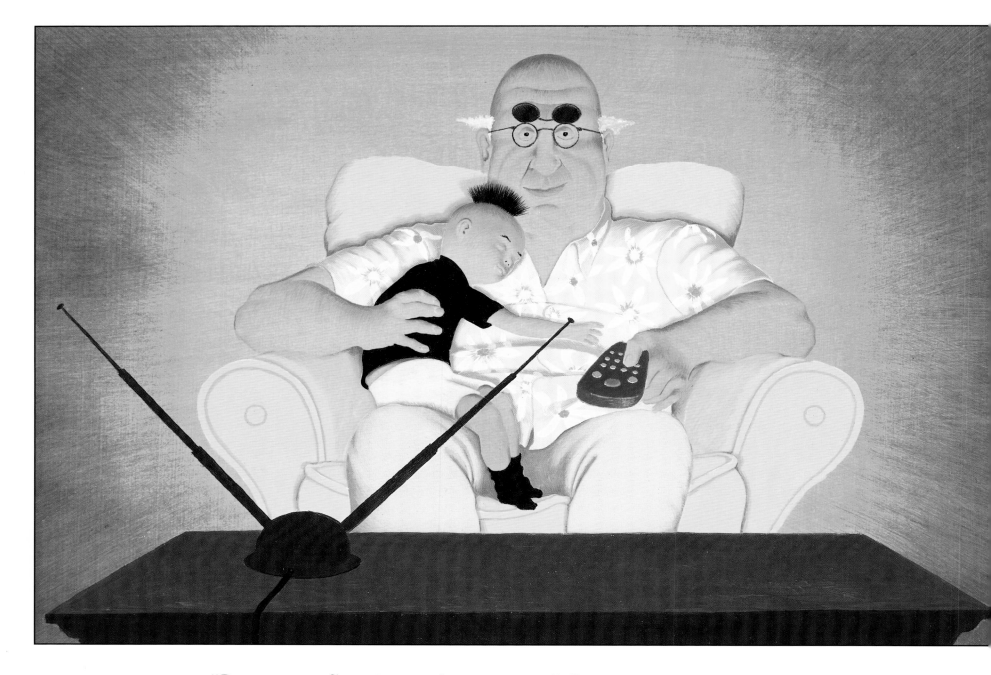

"Remember, Grandpa, only one hour," Rex said, swallowing a
yawn. Later, he'd tell Grandpa all about his adventures. But for
now, it felt good to be safely back at home.

They settled into the big armchair to watch their favorite show.
As the familiar DEEP SEA HUNT music rose, Rex fell sound asleep.

PUPPIES and PIGGIES

CYNTHIA RYLANT

Illustrated by IVAN BATES

Harcourt, Inc. · Orlando   Austin   New York   San Diego   London

www.HarcourtBooks.com

Library of Congress Cataloging-in-Publication Data
Rylant, Cynthia.
Puppies and piggies/Cynthia Rylant; illustrated by Ivan Bates.
p.   cm.
Summary: Rhyming text describes what various animals do and what they love,
as well as a baby who loves his bed and his mother.
[1. Animals—Fiction.   2. Mother and child—Fiction.   3. Stories in rhyme.]
I. Bates, Ivan, ill.   II. Title.
PZ8.3.R96Pu   2008
[E]—dc22   2004003136
ISBN 978-0-15-202321-8

First edition
A C E G H F D B

Manufactured in China

The illustrations in this book were done on
Saunders Waterford paper with wax crayons and watercolors.
The display type was set in Eastman.
The text type was set in Cantoria.
Color separations by Bright Arts Ltd., Hong Kong
Manufactured by South China Printing Company, Ltd., China
Production supervision by Christine Witnik
Designed by Lydia D'moch

For Owen
—C. R.

For Grace
—I. B.

Puppy loves the farmyard,
Puppy loves the rain.

Puppy loves to press his nose
Against the windowpane.

Kitty loves a garden,
Kitty loves a rose.

Kitty loves to walk up high
On her kitty toes.

Bunny loves some lettuce,
Bunny loves some peas.

Bunny loves to hide herself
Among the apple trees.

Piggy loves his mud pen,
Piggy loves his slop.

Piggy loves the barn where he
Can roll around and flop.

Chicky loves her nesting,
Chicky loves her seeds.

Chicky loves to peck all day.
That's all Chicky needs.

Mousey loves to wiggle,
Mousey loves to hide.

Mousey loves a nice dark hole
To put himself inside.

Goosey loves his honking,
Goosey loves his walk.

Goosey loves to find a friend
And talk and talk and talk.

Pony loves a pasture,
Pony loves to run.

Pony loves to stretch her legs
In the summer sun.

Baby loves his blanket,
Baby loves his bed.

Baby loves his mama, who will
Kiss his sleepy head.

Happy piggies, happy puppies,
Happy babies, too.
Happy little lovey-doveys . . .

Just
like
YOU!